Blessings & Joy to You —

3474
CH

JOURNEY TO THE RAINBOW'S END

by

DAVID A. ANDERSON

Illustrated by

DONALD JONES

BUDDYTIME PUBLISHERS
1000 S. MAIN ST., SUITE 644, SALINAS, CA 93901

Lovingly Dedicated

To my sisters and brothers: Suzie, Judy, Dan and Ed
– David

To my wife Rosie and my son Sean
– Don

Books by David A. Anderson and Donald Jones:
WHAT YOU CAN SEE YOU CAN BE!
JOURNEY TO THE RAINBOW'S END

Prints available upon request. Write publisher for free brochure.

JOURNEY TO THE
RAINBOW'S END

This is a story we'd like to share
Of Gregory Duck and Roger Bear...

Once, on a bright sunny day
In a place not far away
From the forest in a warm, grassy field,
Sat two hungry, laughing friends,
Back to back like bookends,
Sharing blueberry muffins for a meal.

"What a time we just had!"
They excitedly said.
"We shared what we knew
And we learned something, too.

"We flew fast and far,
And we made some new friends!
What an exciting adventure
To the rainbow's end!"

Soon they both felt relaxed
While counting clouds on their backs,
And Gregory Duck fell asleep near his friend.
But Roger Bear couldn't slumber.
As he lay there, he remembered
What happened on their
Journey to the rainbow's end.

It was not long ago,

When the moon hung so low

One could climb to the sky on its beams.

As they walked on the beach

The friends felt they could reach

Right up and grab hold of their dreams!

"And they would take us," Roger said,
"To the rainbow's end…
The perfect place to tell you, Gregory,
I'm glad you're my friend."

So Roger Bear and Gregory Duck
Climbed a moonbeam to try their luck,
And floating in a cloud they both found
A shiny golden Cadillac –
With room for two and fins on back –
Hovering with a soft whirring sound.

Gregory tried not to think of crashes,
While Roger adjusted his flying glasses
And tightened the knot on his fluttering scarf.
Then Roger Bear jumped right in,
And Gregory reluctantly followed his friend,
Fastening their seat belts before they took off.

"Where will we go?" cried the duck,
Cringing while trying not to look
At how far away they were from the ground.
Roger said, "Never fear, little friend,
We'll chase that rainbow to its end,
And discover a treasure like we've never found!"

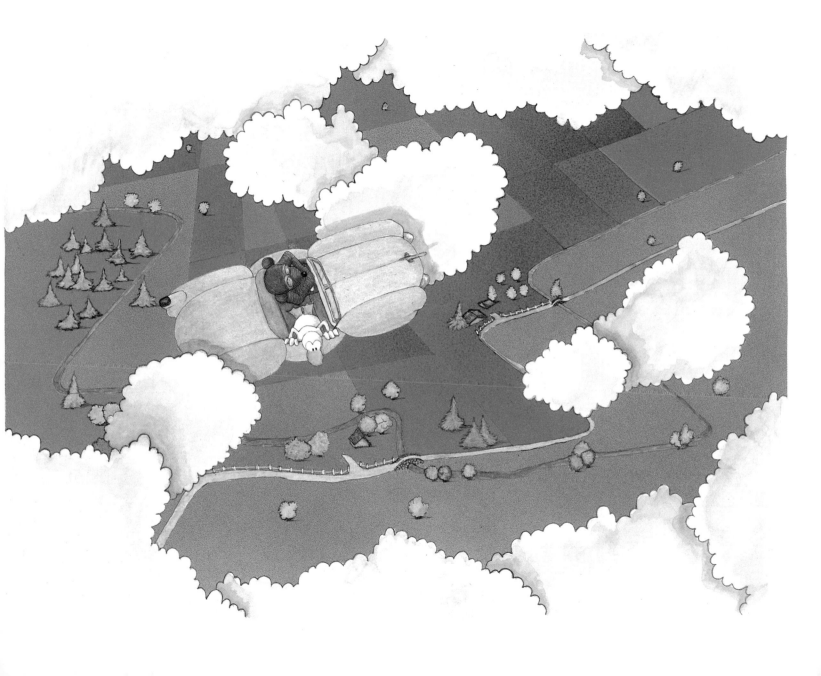

Following the rainbow by its side,
Gregory began to enjoy the ride,
Admiring its many colors and counting the stars.
When it got cold during the flight,
They'd fly through clusters of pearled light
Filling up with just enough to warm their car.

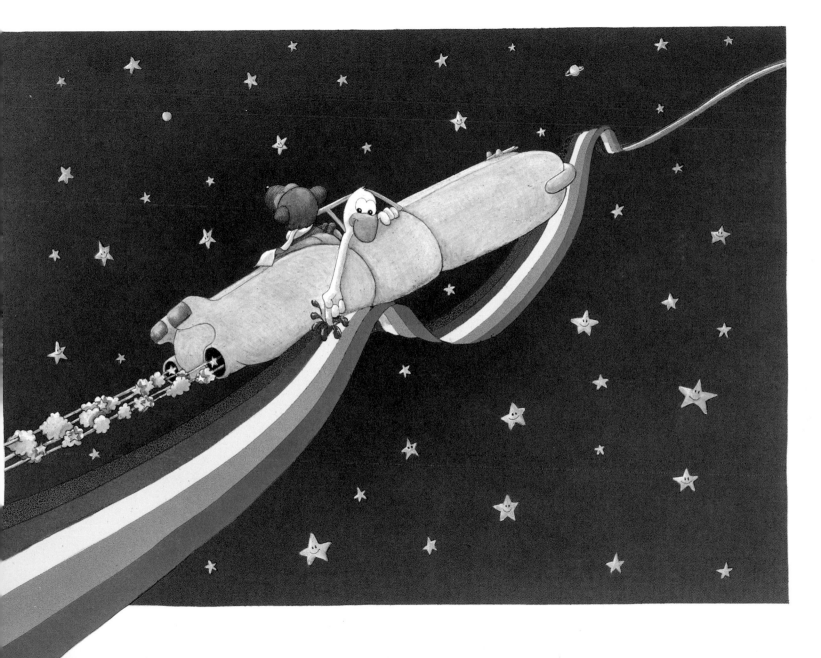

Later, as Roger and Gregory flew
The sky had turned a darker blue,
Though it wasn't really something to fear.
But after squinting and bugging their eyes,
They both began to realize
That one by one the stars would disappear!

Where did they go?
They wanted to know.
What happened to the stars in the sky?
There were blank empty spaces
In front of their faces
With no clues as to how or why.

Then they turned and saw to the right
Something big eating the night
In a great, gulping, chewing fashion.
A giant, flying, frowning whale
Who, with the sweep of an angry tail,
Was turning around and coming right at them!

"Roger, now you turn us around!
Please, get us back to the ground!"
Yelled Gregory, into the space that was cold and hollow.
But before Roger could begin to act,
The great, hungry whale had already attacked,
And the two, along with their car, had been swallowed.

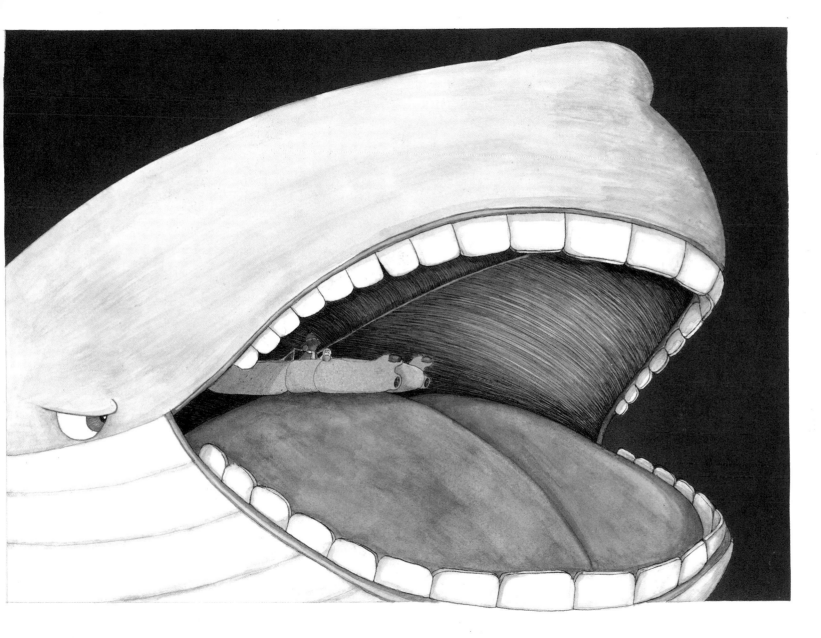

It was quiet and dark inside,
And for the first time on this eventful ride
Neither Roger nor Gregory thought it was fun.
As they looked all about
For a quick, safe way out,
They drove past everything under the sun.

The stars were all there, laying around,
Scared and confused, not making a sound.
Once bright and shiny, now were dimmed by their fear.
So Gregory said to them in a hurry,
"It'll be okay, now don't you worry.
Roger Bear and I will find a way out of here!"

The whale then stopped what he was doing,
Stopped his slurping, gulping and chewing
When Gregory voiced his brave and hopeful words.
Funny, he thought, there was nothing around.
Nothing to make such a little quacking sound.
Yet the whale knew there was something he'd heard.

"Who's that? Who's talking!"
Asked the mighty whale, looking around.
"I'm your friend," answered Gregory,
Who belonged to the little sound.

"I have no friends!" cried the whale, angrily.
"That's why I eat up the sky and all I see!
My life's not full – it's empty and lonely."

Gregory answered, "Stop and think! Please, let go!
You're hurting us – and yourself, if you want to know.
It's not love or friendship or beauty you lack.
If you want love and friendship, try giving it back.
Even when it looks as though it's not there,
First you have to be that love to make it appear.
Know it will return, be deservingly excited!
Because love always comes when so warmly invited.
It may not always look how you expect it to,
But it's love, and it's there, especially for you."

Gregory sat then, quiet and dazed.

Roger watched his little friend, amazed,

Because Gregory wasn't known for public speaking.

But Gregory had let go his fear

Just long enough for all to hear

Perhaps the key to the treasure they were seeking.

The whale responded cheerfully:
"I get it, now I see! The rainbow's end is inside of me!
All the wealth is inside myself!
I'm the pot of gold and all the colors I can be!
All I have to do is receive and give,
Then life can be a joy to live."

"It was and is always your choice,"
Said Gregory's still, calm little voice.

"Okay! Okay! I'll start right away!"
Everyone cheered to hear the whale say,
"Oh boy, it's joy that I choose today!"

Then the whale puckered his lips
And looked around for something to grip,
As he huffed, puffed and pushed at his mighty spout.
He was feeling so happy, that wouldn't you know
In the spirit of loving and letting go
Roger, Gregory and everyone else came tumbling out!

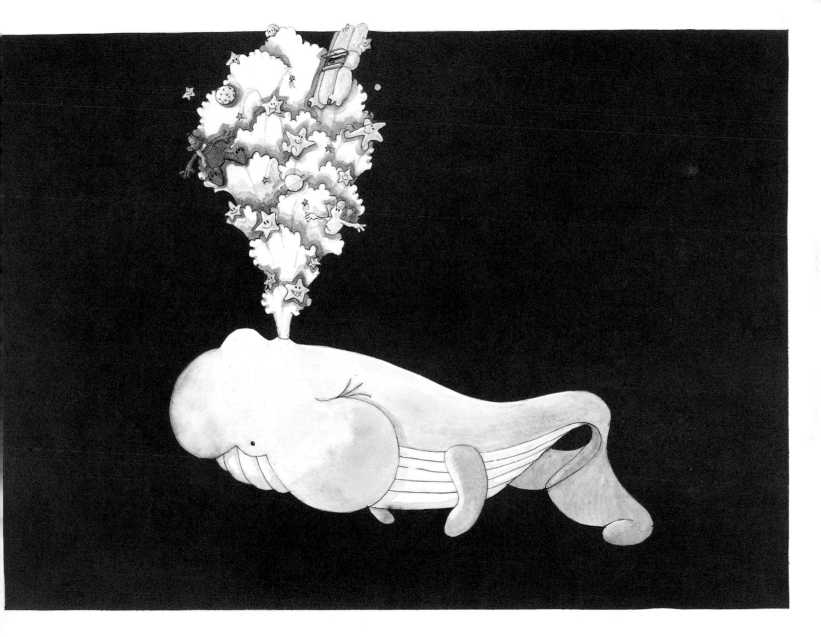

The whale was humbled, cheerful and thankful
To the new friends who were his former tankful,
And he looked brighter and happier from head to tail.
Everyone cheered, laughed and waved
As the whale then turned and swam away,
Leaving a rainbow-colored wake in his trail.

All the stars gleaming again in the sky
Smiled as they passed Roger and Gregory by,
Offering them both a ride on their backs.
"Thank you," Roger warmly said,
"But I think we'll be getting home instead,"
As he patted the dash of the shiny Cadillac.

Roger teased, "Meeting that whale
Was a blessing in disguise.
Who'd have thought
A quiet little duck was so wise?"

Gregory replied, "I think the whale came to show
How to give and receive, how to love and let go."

Then they settled in to enjoy the ride
Because both of them knew deep inside
That their journey had finally come to an end.
And as they sat, every once in a while,
Deep in thought or in the middle of a smile,
They'd say to one another, "I'm glad you're my friend."

Back again in the grassy field,
Where two friends had shared a happy meal,
The sun gave warmth to its neighboring world.
And in that field, lingering there
Were a sleeping duck and a thoughtful bear,
Both lying quietly, slightly curled.

Roger Bear looked at his little friend,

Who had taught him that the rainbow's end

Is inside us all, not something we must seek.

He snuggled up by Gregory's side,

And letting out a contented sigh,

Let his thoughts go, and fell fast asleep.

DAVID ANDERSON grew up in Carmel, California, and lives on a ranch in Monterey County with his wife, Kathee, and triplet sons, Ian, Erik, and Elliot. He enjoys speaking to groups of children and adults, sharing the messages from his books. This is his second book with Don Jones, and more are planned for the future.

DON JONES lives in Carmel, California, with his wife, Rosemary. Don has been illustrating since he was a child, drawing from the people around him. He has been friends with Gregory Duck and Roger Bear for many years. Don's son, Sean, and their dog and cat appear throughout his first book, *What You Can See You Can Be!*